PEACE WALKER

The Legend *of* Hiawatha and Tekanawita

C. J. Taylor

TUNDRA BOOKS

Published in Canada by Tundra Books,
481 University Avenue, Toronto, Ontario M5G 2E9

Published in the United States by Tundra Books of Northern New York,
P.O. Box 1030, Plattsburgh, New York 12901

Library of Congress Control Number: 2004102054

National Library of Canada Cataloguing in Publication

Taylor, C. J. (Carrie J.), 1952-
Peace walker : the legend of Hiawatha and Tekanawita / C.J. Taylor.

ISBN 0-88776-547-5

1. Hiawatha, 15th cent. – Legends.   2. Iroquois Indians – Folklore.
I. Title.

PS8589.A88173P42 2004   J398.2'089'9755   C2004-900840-4

We acknowledge the financial support of the Government of Canada through the Book
Publishing Industry Development Program and that of the Government of Ontario through
the Ontario Media Development Corporation's Ontario Book Initiative. We further
acknowledge the support of the Canada Council for the Arts and the
Ontario Arts Council for our publishing program.

Medium: acrylic on canvas

Printed and bound in Hong Kong, China

1 2 3 4 5 6   09 08 07 06 05 04

IN THE BEGINNING

There remains today evidence of great mound cities that once flourished throughout central North America. Communities expanded quickly around burial mounds and spread over large areas. Slaves and laborers were forced to work for the rich and influential, who were themselves controlled by ruling priests. As time passed, the lands and waterways could no longer support the growing population, and the power of the priests diminished. And so began the great migration. The Iroquois nations – the Onondaga, the Cayuga, the Oneida, the Seneca, and the Mohawk – were among the first peoples to leave their mound city homes.

The five Iroquois nations journeyed northeast in search of a land that could support them, where they could live out their belief in equality and peace. As they moved toward the Great Lakes, the Iroquois split up and formed five separate settlements in territories that had already been settled by the strong, numerous Adirondack. The five nations had grown few and weak from their epic trek. In their weakened state, they fell under the rule of the Adirondack.

For generations, the five nations were forced to pay homage to the Adirondack. But even during the darkest times, they kept the beliefs of their ancestors and longed for freedom. As time passed, the Iroquois people grew stronger and more determined to find the land spoken of in stories of the ancient ones – a land of peace, where homage was paid only to the Creator of the earth, the waters, and skies.

Finally, the time came when, strong in number and spirit, the Iroquois set out from the territory of the Adirondack. Their heavily laden canoes glided northeast, toward the Oswego River. They had almost reached the mouth of the river when they realized that a large party of Adirondack warriors had followed them. The warriors were not burdened with supplies, women, and children, and their war canoes cut swiftly through the waters. The Iroquois could see them coming. They prepared to battle to death, determined not to return to the rule of the Adirondack.

With the war canoes almost upon them, the skies suddenly grew dark. A chilling wind swept across the waters forming huge crashing waves. Black clouds sent down torrents of rain. The ferocious storm raged on, until – just as suddenly as it had started – the skies cleared and the river was again calm. The Iroquois saw before them, in the tranquil waters and along the rocky shoreline, the twisted and battered wreckage of the Adirondack war canoes. Their own canoes were untouched and their people unharmed. At last they were free! Free to make their own homes and live according to their own beliefs. Free to live in peace.

So it was that the territory around the Oswego River became the homeland of the five nations of the Iroquois. The Onondaga, People of the Hills, settled closest to the Oswego River near Onondaga Creek. The Cayuga,

People of the Pipe, settled west of the Onondaga. The Oneida, People of the Standing Stone, built their villages along the shores of Lake Oneida. The Seneca, People of the Great Mountains, settled on the shores of the Canandaigua Lake. The Mohawk held the largest territory, stretching from the northern shore of the St. Lawrence to Stadacona and Hochelaga.

◆ 1 ◆

For generations the five nations lived peacefully and prosperously according to the ways of their ancestors. They developed a clan system that included all the territories. Marriage was forbidden within clans, and when a man married, he joined the clan lodge of his wife.

With time, however, the way of peace vanished. Clan laws permitted victims of injustices, such as theft or even murder, to seek compensation or revenge for the wrongs done to them. But it is difficult to be fair in revenge. Sometimes two lives were taken for one, and thus blood feuds began. Soon it was no longer clan seeking revenge against clan, but nation against nation.

Killing and hatred, suspicion and fear replaced peace. The once well-traveled waterways and trails were no longer safe. Those who did travel carried weapons of war. Clan leaders became greedy for power. They passed sentences of death for the slightest offence. Favors were bought with riches taken in battle and raids. Constant warring became a way of life for so long that no one could remember a time when there had been peace.

It was during these times of chaos that there came into power, in the territories of the Onondaga, a chief named Atotarho. His cruel leadership was to last the span of many lifetimes.

The old ones told stories of a young Chief Atotarho who had stood tall and strong and was a master of magic and wizardry. He had an unquenchable thirst for power, equaled only by his lust for war. His evil sorcery gave him the power to skin walk, changing from human form into that of a giant serpent.

Over time, Atotarho's sturdy proud body had become bent and crooked. Patches of scales covered his skin. His strong hands curled into claws like a bear's. Live snakes wriggled in and out of his gray hair and slithered up and down his scaly arms. His orange eyes could pierce a man's soul

Atotarho's dwelling was not within the stockade walls of the Onondaga settlement, for he trusted no one. Instead, he built his lodge in the swamplands to the south in the Onondaga Creek territory. His longhouse was well guarded by his legion of loyal warriors, all of them blood-thirsty warlords eager to do his bidding. The walls of the swamp lodge were stacked with the bones and skulls of his many victims. Some were decorated and carved into cups and bowls. Others held teeth strung on strips of hide to form necklaces. The fire pit was lined with skulls, their jaws open wide in silent cries. The eye sockets glowered, casting a faint light on the platforms piled high with his many riches.

Atotarho sat among his trophies on a platform built from human bones in a nest of bulrushes woven to fit his crooked body. In one claw, he held the small skull of a child. His medicine cup sat beside the woven nest. It held a secret potion that helped lessen the torturous pain of his twisted body and spirit.

Throughout the entire Iroquois territories there was no one who could oppose his cruel leadership, for Atotarho's spies were everywhere, his warlords quick to respond. The warring and raids, killing and destruction continued until there came a time when the people could tolerate no more.

In an Onondaga village, three days' travel from Atotarho's swampy domain, there was but one man brave enough to stand in defiance. Chief Hiawatha had once been a great warrior himself, loyal to Atotarho. He had led many successful raids, fought many battles, and had been granted many favors. But he no longer had the heart for battle or war. He spoke of peace.

Atotarho's spies soon learned of Hiawatha's refusal to follow or enforce Atotarho's evil orders. When the spies reported back to him, Atotarho thought of the favors and privileges he had granted Hiawatha over the years and he was enraged at being repaid with defiance.

A sharp blade of pain racked Atotarho's body. He reached for his medicine cup, drank the bitter brew, and let the cup fall to the floor. He could hear the sounds of his warriors outside, questioning a captive. Easing himself deeper into his nest, he summoned a young slave hidden in the shadows.

"Fill my cup and send in the fools I hear," he ordered, his voice shaking the rafters of the longhouse. The boy rushed forward to fill the cup from the large clay pot he carried and quickly left.

The warriors pushed aside the hide covering the doorway and entered the dim longhouse, allowing daylight to stream in with them. Atotarho raised his crooked arm to cover his eyes.

The two fearsome warriors stood before the fire pit, a young bound captive cowering between their enormous tattooed bodies. The bone platform creaked as Atotarho eased himself forward, his orange eyes glaring. "I do not have the patience for this," he thundered. "Bring me this slave's head. Send the rest of him back to his family. Tell them, 'serve me in life, or serve me in death. It is of no matter to me.'" Before they could leave, he shouted one more order. "Tell the chiefs I will hold council when next the moon is full. Go now!"

The warriors and their doomed captive backed away. Again the hide covering the door flapped open and the flash of daylight sent sharp shards of pain into Atotarho's head. The snakes slithered in and out of his tangled gray hair, faster and faster as if they felt the agony that danced around inside his skull.

Alone in his nest amid his dreadful trophies, once more Atotarho grabbed his medicine cup in one bear-claw hand while the other clumsily held the small child's skull. He drained the bitter liquid and fell back into his woven cradle. Holding the tiny skull tightly to his heaving chest, he looked deep into the empty eye sockets. He began to speak in a voice unlike the one that had barked orders, a voice more like that of a young child. "What shall we do with this man Hiawatha? This man I have granted many favors, who served me well but now opposes me." Atotarho gazed at the empty stare. "I think death is too easy. It is better to watch him. He will show us others who are disloyal." Atotarho's voice grew softer. "Yes, my young friend, for now it is best to watch Hiawatha. Yes, watch – very closely."

◆ 2 ◆

Grandmother Moon shone brightly on the night that the Onondaga leaders gathered at Atotarho's swampy domain. Two large warriors stood guard before the doorway removing the men's weapons as they meekly filed into the smoky lodge. An eerie orange light flickered in the empty eye sockets of the skulls that ringed the fire pit. Sparks shot silent screams from their open mouths. The men sat in silence, heads bowed, and felt that another pair of orange eyes watched their every move and read their every thought.

From the shadows the bone platform creaked. Atotarho leaned forward. "Cowards," he whispered to the tiny skull in his bear-claw hand. "No one is brave enough to look upon me."

Atotarho was about to bark his first command when the hide was pulled open. All heads turned to see who was foolish enough or brave enough to interrupt the fearsome Atotarho. There stood Chief Hiawatha.

He was of average height and solid build. Although he had seen many battles, he had few scars. None had touched his handsome face or distorted

his tattoos. He refused to shave his head as the other warriors did, and his hair was long and brightly decorated with blue feathers. He wore fine, fur-lined robes, a deer-hide shirt, leggings, and moccasins. All were fashioned and decorated by his beloved daughters.

Hiawatha looked calmly at the glaring orange stare and the lowered heads of the seated men. "Excuse my interruption, Chief Atotarho. Please continue."

Atotarho grabbed his medicine cup, he threw back his head, and drained the numbing liquid. When he looked again, Hiawatha was no longer standing in the doorway. He was seated among the men.

"Do you fools think I do not know there are those among you who defy me? We will see how far this will go. My warlords are to prepare for raids. They will take every man who can hold a weapon. They will take the supplies they need. They will head north to the territory of the Huron. Raid their villages, burn their lodges, kill everyone!"

Pain wrapped around Atotarho's rib cage with each breath. He stopped speaking and leaned back, gasping for air. No one moved as they watched the tiny child's skull ride up and down on his heaving chest.

Finally the heaving and gasping ended. "Go home and prepare for my war chiefs to instruct you. I will tolerate no defiance." His orange eyes looked into those of Hiawatha. "From anyone."

There was nothing to do but to follow the Chief's orders. His wrath was far worse than battle.

And so the warring continued. The people lived in hopelessness and despair. Atotarho's loyal disciples enforced his whims. They ravaged the people and they ravaged the earth. So many had been dragged off to serve as warriors or slaves or to be killed that few were left to tend the gardens or hunt for what little game was left. The meager crops that were harvested were taken or burned as punishment. Entire forests were burnt to the ground, leaving the animals as homeless as the people. Soon there was nothing left to lose.

A few brave souls sought the counsel of Hiawatha. One night they held a secret meeting in the turtle lodge of the Onondaga village, three days' travel north of Chief Atotarho's swamp lodge. Under cover of darkness, the people gathered at the hearth of Hiawatha and his seven beloved daughters. A cloud of hopelessness enveloped them. The longhouse was filled with an empty silence.

One of Hiawatha's daughters stood up and threw a dry piece of wood into the fire pit. The flames leaped and crackled, throwing light on the hides that divided the many hearths down the center of the lodge.

The man who had been chosen to speak cleared his throat. "We came for your help, Hiawatha. You are the only one brave enough to defeat Atotarho. We look to you to end this madness." The man lowered his head. This was not the speech he had prepared, but one he gave in desperation.

One by one, each person told of loss. Across the fire pit, surrounded by his daughters, Hiawatha sat and listened to the tales of sorrow and grief. When all had finished, they waited in silence.

Hiawatha began to speak. "Like you, I no longer have the heart for war. But I am one man. I cannot end this evil alone. We must stand together as one mind, one spirit, one people. Only then can we overcome Atotarho's reign"

In desperation, they agreed to follow Hiawatha.

There was much discussion and planning that night in the turtle lodge. Finally, with everything settled, Hiawatha spoke one last time. "Go home and prepare for three days of travel and try to rest. Tomorrow, as the sun rises, we will gather where the river and the pathway meet. Some of you will travel by canoe. I will lead the others along the pathway to the swamplands and Atotarho's lodge. Together we will stand before him. One mind. One spirit. One people.

While the people returned to their lodges filled with hope, Atotarho's spies were paddling north, their strong arms plying the waters in unison.

As soon as the sun had risen over the rolling hills, the people began their trek. Some paddled their canoes on the tranquil waters of the river. The others followed Hiawatha on foot along a trail that rose over rock cliffs and jutted high above the deep water.

Although the sun was warm and the nights mild, after three days they had grown weak from hunger and fatigue. Hiawatha, with his long stride, was soon far ahead of the others. When he reached the large boulders at the mouth of a swamp, he waited as the canoes glided toward him and those on foot descended the cliff trail.

As Hiawatha watched the others approach, the clear blue skies suddenly grew dark. A cold violent wind rose and churned the tranquil waters into crashing waves. He watched helplessly as the waters turned and twisted, swallowing up canoes, smashing the shoreline, and washing away chunks of the rocky cliffs. The wind and waters swirled up into dark angry clouds that spit jagged bolts of light. With each flash came a terrible cry. A large black hole had formed in the clouds. The cry came again. Closer and closer, louder and louder.

In another flash of light, Hiawatha heard an agonized shriek and saw a great giant serpent twisting and turning through the river. Its huge scaly head was alive with snakes that swarmed madly about him. From its wide mouth twitched a long red tongue.

The next flash of light did not bring a cry of pain, but a thunderous voice. "Hiawatha, go back to the village. See how many are left to follow you."

The serpent recoiled into the gaping black hole in the sky.

Once again, Atotarho's powerful wizardry had terrorized the people into fearful submission.

◆ 4 ◆

The people were too afraid of Atotarho's wrath to seek Chief Hiawatha's council again. In desperation, they sought the council of the great Seer, for he was able to unveil the future and was much respected among the five nations.

The Seer lived in a shabby shelter deep in the woods that lined a small river a day's walk from the Onanadaga village. While he waited for the elders to arrive, Seer prepared for council. He stood at the river's edge and gave thanks for his gift of sight, then he plunged into the cleansing waters. When he waded out of the river, a chilling northern wind swept through the trees and across the water. Droplets ran down from the wispy strands of white hair that age had left upon his head. Shivers rattled his frail old frame as he reached the shore. He welcomed the warmth of the white feather cloak that lay on the sun-warmed rock. He wrapped it tightly around his bony shoulders and, pulling the hood up over his wet hair, he followed the path to his lodge and to the elders who awaited him.

The elders sat huddled around the smoldering fire pit in the tiny shelter. Blue-white smoke circled them, misting their vision and burning their eyes. The air was thick with dampness, filled with the smell of moldy skins, drying plants, and rotting meat. Suddenly, from the vale of smoke, there appeared a giant white bird. It held a turtle rattle and sang as it circled the fire pit, coming to rest on a pile of rotting hides. Seer let his white feather cloak drop in a heap around his crossed legs. Even without the cloak he resembled a giant old bird. His long hooked nose sat between deep eyes shadowed by wiry white eyebrows. He wore a necklace of carved bone feathers. His bare bony shoulders looked like folded wings. There was a long silence before he began to speak.

"I have seen, in my dreams, a man. He is Huron, from the north. He walks with peace in his heart. This man travels east to the Mohawk. He waits for Chief Hiawatha. Together they will bring an end to the wars. Together they will prevail." Seer paused and looked at the elders. "Hiawatha must leave his village and travel to the Mohawk. These two men must come together."

The elders knew that Hiawatha would never leave his beloved daughters or his responsibility to the people as their chief. He would have to be driven from the village.

There lived in the lands of the Iroquois an evil shaman named Osinoh. He was a despicable little man who resembled an owl. His short fat arms and legs were attached to a round ball of a body. His head sat atop his shoulders making it seem that he had no neck. He stood no higher than the waist of an average man. Osinoh enjoyed using his powers and magic to torment the minds and souls of his victims. The elders were desperate: they would ask Osinoh to find a way to drive Hiawatha from the village.

One night, Osinoh perched on a tree branch overlooking the turtle lodge of Hiawatha and his seven daughters. He sang in the voice of a screech owl. Calling the name of Hiawatha's youngest daughter, he cried, "Marry me, Cloud Dancer, or you will die!"

He sang throughout the night. In the morning Osinoh climbed down and hid in the forest. Within three days the young girl was dead. Hiawatha was heart broken, yet none of his people came to comfort him. They were too ashamed at having caused such grief.

Osinoh made five more nightly visits. Each time he sang to another daughter. Each time the young girl died. Hiawatha's sorrow was close to madness. His grieving cries were heard throughout the village, yet no one came to console him.

One last time Osinoh climbed the tree and sang his death song, naming Hiawatha's only remaining daughter. Her death sent Hiawatha into the dark depths of madness. He sat alone before his cold lifeless hearth. In his mind he heard the voices and laughter of his dear daughters. He saw Jay's joyful smile and heard her chatter as she groomed and decorated his long black hair with beautiful blue feathers. He saw his oldest daughter, Rain, moving about gracefully as she prepared the evening meal of deer meat and corn stew. The voices of Tracker and Deer Caller echoed through his mind as they spoke of the hunt. He could smell the colored mixtures that Painter used to decorate the fine robe he wore. He saw Looks Again hunched over her quill-work as Cloud Dancer sang and swirled around her sisters.

Still no one came to comfort him. In his terrible grief he cried out, "Nothing is left! My daughters have been taken from me. My people have turned away from me. I can no longer live in this village. I will live as a woodsman, alone in the forest." The whole village heard his cries. The elders knew that Osinoh had done his dreadful work: Hiawatha had been driven away.

The people watched that night as Hiawatha left his empty turtle lodge. He had not yet reached the stockade gate that led to the forest when Atotarho's warlords set fire to his lodge. Great orange flames crackled and leaped skyward. Thick black smoke drifted over the high walls of the stockade fence and through the trees surrounding the village. Hiawatha did not look back.

So it was that, robed in grief, Hiawatha left his village on the Oswego River. Blindly, he followed the trail that led north toward the mountains. He walked until his legs could no longer carry him. He fell to the ground and slept where he lay.

Each day he wandered, feeling neither hunger nor thirst. He felt only the dark pain of the loss of his daughters. Finally he collapsed with exhaustion.

After a long sleep, Hiawatha awoke to find that he had crossed the mountains and was on the edge of marshland. It was overgrown with strange round and jointed rushes. Without thought, he gathered some of the reeds and built a fire. That night he sat by his campfire and made three strings from the hollow, beadlike reeds. Holding the strands up, he spoke aloud.

"With these shells I would offer condolence to those who suffer as I do. I would lift the darkness of sorrow from them."

The next day, Hiawatha's journey took him east to the shores of a small lake. A large flock of ducks covered its surface. There were so many ducks that Hiawatha could not see the water. He cried out, "If I am truly a powerful leader, allow these fowl to rise up and lift the waters so I may walk across on dry land."

Suddenly, with a great flapping of wings, the ducks flew skyward, lifting the waters of the lake. Hiawatha saw before him the dry lake bed. Spread over the lake bed were layers of the small white and purple shell of the water snail. As he crossed, he gathered the shells. When he reached the far shore, Hiawatha watched as the ducks descended from the clouds and replaced the water of the lake.

That evening he felt hunger for the first time. He hunted and prepared three ducks to roast over his campfire. As the aroma of roasting duck filled the air, Hiawatha removed his shirt and unraveled the thin strips of leather that held the seams. The hide was soft and supple, the quillwork exquisite. Tears clouded his eyes as he worked. "Forgive me, daughters, for I need the thongs to string and make a pouch to hold these precious shells." When he was finished, he ate his meal and found the strength to continue on his journey.

When the sun rose, he returned to the trail that led north. At twilight he came upon a clearing. He could see that it had once been a village garden but now it bore the mark of Atotarho. Across the burnt ground and charred crops was a tiny field lodge that had somehow stayed standing. It offered little shelter, for there was no hide to cover the doorway and the roof had many holes. All that remained inside were a few pieces of dry firewood. Hiawatha built a small fire. In the tangle of wood he found three straight poles. He erected two of the poles and placed the third across the top. From it he hung the three strands of shells.

Across the burnt clearing in the dark shadows, a little girl, not more than eleven summers, watched the stranger in the shabby field lodge. She held a woven basket half full of a few salvaged vegetables. She could hear him

speaking yet saw that he sat alone. The girl left her basket and crept closer. The man was kneeling before three strands of shells suspended from a pole. His voice was filled with sadness as he said the same words over and over: "With these shells, I would console those in sorrow." The girl quietly retrieved her basket and hurried back to the village.

When she entered her lodge she cried, "Father, there is a stranger in the old field lodge. He speaks to strands of shells, the same words over and over."

"Slow down, child, you are making no sense," said her father.

When her mother saw the basket the girl carried, she was angry. "You were told not to wander into the clearing!"

"I am sorry, Mother, but I found a few things for the cooking skin. The little ones are crying from hunger, and I thought that perhaps the warriors' fire may have spared some of the crops. I found corn and a few beans and two squashes. As I was about to come home, I saw a light in the old field lodge. Inside sat a stranger. His hair was long and covered with blue feathers. He wore a fine robe decorated with giant turtles."

The girl drew a breath and continued. "The man was kneeling before shells suspended from a pole. He said, 'with these shells, I would console those in sorrow,' again and again."

"This stranger must be Chief Hiawatha," said her father. Since he was driven from his village, he wanders the woodlands. Some say he is mad. I will send a messenger to invite him to join our evening council."

The messenger returned the next day with news that Hiawatha had accepted the invitation. That evening Chief Hiawatha sat among the people. For days and days he listened to their talk. Suspicion and jealousy fueled their words. Not once was Hiawatha called upon for his advice.

Discouraged, he left the council and the village. He found the first path outside the stockade walls and once again he wandered the woodlands until exhaustion overtook him. Once again he built a fire and once again he erected the poles. He spoke to the strands of shells. "Should I see anyone in grief, I would console them. I would lift the blanket of sorrow from their hearts."

The smoke from Hiawatha's campfire rose to the sky. There was a Mohawk village nearby, and a spy was sent to report back to the chief. "Surely the smoke must come from the campfire of Chief Hiawatha, one of the great men of the Seer's dream. He is to meet the man from the north," said the chief. "Go and tell this man that our village welcomes him."

Hiawatha returned to the village with the spy. For several days he joined their council and listened to the people argue and argue, never coming to agreement. Disheartened, he was preparing to leave when he was summoned by the chief. A runner had arrived with an important message from a village to the east on the Mohawk River.

◆ 6 ◆

On the shores of a great lake to the north lay the territory of the Huron. Like the Iroquois, they had suffered the cruel brutality of Atotarho's whims. Many Huron villages had been destroyed, food stores stolen, fields and lodges burned. The captured were tortured to death or enslaved. Babies and young children were stolen and raised as Atotarho's disciples.

The Huron themselves began to take on the habits of the warlike Iroquois. They lived in constant fear and suspicion. Bitterness ate at their hearts. Jealousy and greed led to senseless fighting. Misery was a way of life.

On a hill overlooking a large sweeping bay on the northern tip of the great lake was one such ravaged Huron village. There lived a man unlike the other people of his village. He was set apart even before his birth. When his mother was pregnant, she had gone into a long sleep. In her dream, a messenger spoke to her about the son to whom she would soon give birth. "Name the child Tekanawita. Someday he will journey to the lands of the Mohawk. There he will be recognized as a great man. He will meet another great man of the Onondaga. Together they will plant the Tree of Peace."

When she heard of the dream, his grandmother feared the child and the wrath of Atotarho. "As soon as he is born, you must drown him," said the grandmother. When the infant was born, her obedient daughter took him to the frozen bay. She chopped a hole in the ice and threw him in. But that night she awoke to find the infant sleeping next to her. Once again she took the baby to the frozen bay and threw him in. And again she awoke to find the infant beside her.

"I will do the deed myself," said the grandmother when her daughter told her what had happened. She took the child to the bay and threw him into a hole hacked in the ice. The next morning she found the child nestled close to his mother.

"Daughter, this child is special for he cannot be drowned," said the grandmother. "He will become a great man. Take care in raising him."

When he was a boy, the other children thought that Tekanawita was peculiar. They taunted and teased him for his gentle ways. He grew into a handsome, gentle man who had no love for war. Many seasons passed, and the people's hearts grew more bitter as they suffered abuse themselves. Finally they drove the gentle Tekanawita from the village and the land of the Huron.

Tekanawita's mother was very old. Leaving her meant that he would not see her again.

"Do not worry about me, my son. I was told before your birth of this day. You are a great man. You must journey to the territory of the Mohawk and Onondaga. There you will plant the Tree of Peace."

His mother watched silently as Tekanawita prepared his travel bundle. He spread out the tattered hide and on it he placed a small skinning knife, a leather pouch containing dried meat and berries, and another containing sacred tobacco. Before he could roll up and tie the bundle, his mother handed him a new pair of moccasins. Tucked inside were bunches of strings. "Take these. You have a long path ahead. The strings will be useful for mending."

That night Tekanawita's journey began. He paddled across the great lake and into the hunting territories of the Mohawk. By dawn he had reached the mouth of the Mohawk River. Tekanawita's canoe glided up the quiet river as the night mist swirled up from the water and tree-lined shore and melted into the morning sun. He came to a sandy beach a few paces from a waterfall and pulled his canoe up on shore so that he could make camp and rest.

Tekanawita sat before his small campfire and threw a pinch of sacred tobacco onto the flames. Puffs of gray smoke floated up, carrying his prayers. A passing hunter noticed the smoke. He approached cautiously, but when he saw that the odd stranger carried no weapons, he hurried back to his village and reported to his chiefs.

A delegation was sent to question the stranger. The oldest of the chiefs was the chosen speaker. "Who are you and where do you come from?"

"I am Huron. My people live at the northern tip of the great lake. My name is Tekanawita."

"What is your purpose here?" asked the old chief.

"I have come to end the wars so that you will no longer live in misery." Tekanawita continued, "It was told in a dream to my mother before my birth."

The old chief looked about at the others in the council. "We have heard stories of a gifted dreamer of the Onondaga. A man named Seer. His dreams told of a man from the Huron Nation to the north who walks with peace in his heart. It is said that the man is to meet with the great chief of the

Onondaga, Hiawatha. Together they will bring peace to all the Iroquois people. Are you that man?"

"I am that man," said Tekanawita.

"How can we be certain?" asked the chief.

"As an infant I could not be drowned. Choose the manner of my death and you will see that if my purpose is true, I cannot die now," said Tekanawita.

The delegation talked about ways in which they could test Tekanawita by trying to put him to death. None wanted Tekanawita's blood on his hands. Finally, the old chief stepped forward. He pointed to the canyon cliffs above the waterfall. There grew a pine tree, the tallest and oldest anyone had ever seen.

"Climb to the highest branch and jump down into the canyon. No man could survive such a fall."

All watched as Tekanawita climbed to the tree top. He wavered for but a moment and plunged into the dark depths of the canyon. The members of the delegation were certain that he was dead. They returned to the village.

The next morning, smoke rose from Tekanawita's campfire. The delegation once again made its way into the forest to the foot of the cliffs. They found Tekanawita seated by his fire, eating his morning meal. It was then that they knew that he was the man from the Seer's dream.

◆ 7 ◆

Hiawatha entered through the high stockade wall that surrounded the Mohawk village, followed closely by a chief and five fearsome warriors who had been sent to keep him safe. A delegation of chiefs stood waiting before the largest longhouse. An old man wrapped in a fur robe stepped forward to greet the party. "What is your business here?" he asked.

"I have come to meet with the man from the north," said Hiawatha.

"He awaits your arrival," said the chief. Turning to the party that accompanied Hiawatha, he said, "Return to your territory. Give thanks to your leaders for Hiawatha's safe arrival. Tell them that the two great men are together. Let them now establish peace."

Two small children peeked out from behind the hide-covered door. When they saw the old chief lead the man toward the lodge, they scurried back to their grandmother. "He comes! He comes! The great Onondaga chief is here!" they cried.

All heads turned toward the doorway. Suddenly the hide was thrown open and light flooded the lodge. Tekanawita, who had been sitting among the people lining the walls of the smoke-filled longhouse, stood up.

"Welcome, young brother!" he said to Hiawatha. "I know of your pain and loss. Come share my fire so we may speak together."

When they were seated by the fire, Hiawatha began his tale. He told of the evil Osinoh, of how his daughters had died, and of how his people had turned away from him in his grief. "They turn from each other. Over and over I see only accusations, suspicion, and revenge in their hearts."

"There is to be another council," said Tekanawita. "I will return and tell you what they reply."

That evening everyone gathered at the longhouse to hear Tekanawita speak, but Hiawatha sat alone in the lodge. He untied his shirt bundle and took out the poles. When he had set them up in the usual fashion, he knelt down and hung the three strands of shells. As he placed each strand he said, "With these shells I would console those who are covered in sorrow."

He sat back on his heels and thought aloud, "It is useless. The people feel nothing of one another's sorrows. All they do is accuse and avenge."

When the council was over, Tekanawita appeared in the doorway of Hiawatha's lodge and listened to his words. "Brother, I see now the torment you carry," said Tekanawita. "I will help remove the darkness that covers you. We need clear minds and hearts if we are to have peace. Do you have any more shells?"

Hiawatha reached for the pouch that held the shells he had gathered from the dry lake bed. The shells spilled out. "I have many shells but no strings," he said.

Tekanawita remembered the strings inside the moccasins in his travel bundle. He smiled. "I have strings. With your permission I will string more shell strands for your pole. And with these we shall mend your heart and mind."

When all the shell strands were finished and the words spoken, the darkness was lifted and Hiawatha was consoled.

"Young brother, your mind and heart are clear now, so we can establish a Great Peace, a peace that will end the wars and bring the brothers and sisters of all the nations together.

"But what of Atotarho?" said Hiawatha. "His wicked spirit will never agree to such a peace."

"When this union of nations is established, we will compose a Peace Song and journey to the lodge of Atotarho."

8

A young man left the Mohawk village on the Mohawk River. When he had paddled as far as the waterways flowed, he left his canoe. On foot, he followed the trails that led to the Oswego River, traveling night and day with no rest. He reached the Onondaga village after nightfall. Silently, he crept through the woods that surrounded the high stockade wall to the river. Stealing a canoe, he continued south toward the marshland at the mouth of the river. After three days, as the sun reached the center of the sky, the canoe glided into the swampy realm of Atotarho.

Two sentries stepped forward. "What is your business?" demanded one of them.

"My name is Racer. I come with important information for the chief," said the young man as he beached his canoe.

One of the guards escorted Racer to Atotarho. Racer entered the lodge, careful to let in as little light as possible. Nevertheless, a screech of agony came from the dark shadows across the skull-lined fire pit. As Racer's eyes adjusted to the murky light, he saw the platform and the woven nest that held Atotarho's twisted body. His orange eyes glared at the terrified young man. "Is your news important enough to disturb our rest?" roared Atotarho. He turned his eyes to the child's skull he cupped lovingly in his bear-claw hand.

"I come from the Mohawk territory on the Mohawk River. In the village near the falls, the two men of Seer's dream sit together. The man from the north has lifted the madness from Hiawatha's mind." He fell silent, afraid to continue.

The bone platform groaned as Atotarho reached for his medicine cup. "Do not try my patience. Tell me all you know."

"They speak of a Great Peace." Racer cleared his throat. "And the people listen."

"I will not abide their defiance!" Atotarho cried. The lodge was full of dark silence. "Return to the village and watch them. Go now, leave us alone."

Racer watched the tormented creature turn to the tiny skull and, in a childlike voice, murmur, "We will decide what is to be done."

Racer hurried from the lodge and back to his canoe. He paddled with all his strength, leaving behind the swamp lodge and Chief Atotarho's dreadful rage.

The Mohawk village was so busy with people coming and going and preparing for the many meetings, that nobody had noticed Racer's long absence. Tekanawita and Hiawatha were to speak at council that evening. All the chiefs of the Mohawk territories had been invited. Everyone was to attend.

That night, the people listened to the words of the two great men. Tekanawita was the first to speak. "We have invited the chiefs of these territories to hear our plan and to see their opinion. We ask for their consent to proceed. We must establish a union of all nations. The laws of the confederacy must have full agreement. Each nation will be represented by chiefs of great virtue, honesty, and patience."

Tekanawita and Hiawatha continued to explain what was needed. Finally, when all had been said, the chiefs expressed their agreement. Messengers would go to each territory so that everyone could consider Tekanawita and Hiawatha's plan.

The messengers went first to the Oneida. Four seasons passed before their return with news. The Oneida would join the union of nations. Next, the messengers were sent to the Onondaga nation. Again they returned within four seasons. The Onondaga would join the union. As would the people of the Cayuga nation. Among the Seneca chiefs there was indecision. Two cycles of seasons passed until they agreed to join the confederacy. Tekanawita and Hiawatha had worked for five cycles of seasons to bring the Iroquois nations together in agreement.

There remained only one in opposition to the Great Peace. Atotarho.

Once again the two great men sought the council of the chiefs. Tekanawita spoke. "My younger brother, Hiawatha, and I have composed a song. It is a song of peace, one that will console the twisted soul and body of Atotarho. Unless he changes, we can never find the Great Peace. We ask that messengers be sent to all the nations with invitations to join us. When all have learned and can sing the song of peace together, we will seek out Atotarho."

The chiefs sent messengers that very day. From across the vast territories, the people followed the mountain trails, woodland paths, and waterways that led to the village where the two great men of Seer's dream waited.

When the multitudes had gathered at the Mohawk village on the Mohawk River near the falls, the chiefs of all the nations called council. The meeting

was held in the Bear Lodge. It was the largest longhouse in the stockade, yet it could not contain all the people. Inside, Tekanawita and Hiawatha sat among the many chiefs that surrounded the smoky fire pit. There was much talking and whispering as they waited for the speaker to begin.

At last an old man stood up, and silence slowly filled the longhouse. When all was still he addressed Tekanawita and Hiawatha. "The laws of our union that you have laid before us have brought us together in peace. There is but one chief who remains, Chief Atotarho. Many still fear him. We wish to send two spies so we may know what awaits us.

With all in agreement, volunteers came forward. First, two tall, lean men moved out of the crowded shadows. "I am Heron and this is Crane," said one of them. "We will go to face Atotarho."

Tekanawita spoke softly. "All here know your love of fishing. Many urgent messages are forgotten along the shoreline of a well stocked river." Heron and Crane looked at each other and stepped back into the crowd.

The next two stepped forward, their short round bodies attesting to their reputation for endless appetites. "You will miss too many meals, my friends," said Tekanawita. The next two men were not suitable either, for they were too timid. And two boys, so alike that they shared one name – Two Crow – bounded forward. They were well known for their mischievous ways.

Before Tekanawita could speak to them, a giant of a man stood up. He wrapped the boys in his huge arms and set them down in the crowd. Turning to face Tekanawita, he spoke. "My name is Bear, and my friend Deer and I will go." The man called Deer rose and stood beside him.

Everyone waited for Tekanawita's answer. "We will wait for your report. Have a safe journey," he said.

9

Bear and Deer reached the marshlands of Atotarho. Their canoe skimmed over the water through the morning mist that clung to the reeds. Their every nerve on edge, their paddles silently split the water and pushed them toward the fearsome lodge.

As they floated closer, the men heard screams that were muffled by the rising mist, but they saw no one. The once heavily guarded lodge seemed deserted. Bear and Deer banked their canoe on the shore. Nervously they crept up to the bulrush lodge. The cries grew louder. They came from inside the lodge.

"Send me one of my guards!" The voice thundered. "Why do I not have news of the two men and those who defy me?"

Bear and Deer pressed against the wall of the lodge. A young slave girl struggled to carry a large clay pot through the narrow doorway. They heard her voice trying to calm the tortured beast that sat in the woven nest atop the bone platform.

"There is no one left," she said. "I have brewed a stronger tea."

Peeking inside the tiny opening, Bear and Deer saw the young girl pour the tea from the clay pot into the medicine cup. As she held it toward the shadows of the platform, the two frightened men saw a massive bear-claw hand grasp the cup. They heard great gulping noises. The girl spoke again. "Everyone has gone to hear the men of Seer's dream. Sleep now. I will wake you if there is news." Bear and Deer had heard and seen enough. They slipped back to the water's edge and turned their canoe to the Mohawk village.

When the chiefs had heard their report of the abandoned Atotarho, they knew that the time had come to journey to the Onondaga territories.

Now, Tekanawita had taught the Peace Song to the people gathered at the Mohawk village. Certain singers were chosen to lead them through the territories. Singing in unison, the people traveled to the Onondaga territory to face Atotarho.

At last the multitude stood before the lodge deep in the swamp. As the chosen singer grew tired, he was replaced with another. Tekanawita saw the man begin to hesitate, so he took his place and, with Hiawatha by his side, he led the people in the Peace Song.

Suddenly a great light filled the swamp. It shone brightest over the reed shelter, dissolving the roof and walls until only the bone platform and its woven nest were left standing.

Tekanawita stepped forward and, as he sang, light poured over the hideous form within the woven nest. He passed his hands over the twisted spirit and tortured body. In another burst of light the wriggling snakes crawled out of Atotarho's tangled hair and dissolved in the brightness. The scales fell from his skin and the bent body began to straighten. His hands were again the hands of a man. Atotarho heard the voices of the people

singing. They sang together as one voice, one mind, one spirit, one people.

And so it was that Atotarho was healed. His body was straight and strong. His horrid nest and platform had been transformed into a giant pine tree, its branches reaching up into the blue white light. Atotarho stood between Tekanawita and Hiawatha under its spreading branches.

Finally the singing voices grew silent and the Great Peace was upon them all.

Hiawatha and Tekanawita stood together under the sheltering branches of the pine tree. Its limbs burst with new green needles. The people waited in silence to hear their words.

Hiawatha began. "To establish this unity of peace among the brothers and sisters of these five nations, we ask the women to present their chosen leaders." Tekanawita continued. "These leaders must be of great virtue and wisdom, for they will be advisors to the people. They must work in unity, never considering their own interests. They must work for the benefit of the people and those not yet born."

The chosen leaders came forward to sit in council under the great tree. Each of them presented Hiawatha and Tekanawita with a string of purple and white lake shells as a pledge of truth. Together they devised the laws and rules that would govern the people in peace. And so were born the Great Peace and the Confederacy of the Five Nations.

THE IROQUOIS CONFEDERACY

The Hau de no sau nee, the People of the Longhouse, trace their great Confederacy back more than 1,500 years, making it one of the oldest continuous forms of government and one of the oldest democracies on Earth.

The original five nations were divided into two groups. The Mohawk, Onondaga, and Seneca made up the Elder; and the Oneida and Cayuga were the Younger. They were all united in one symbolic longhouse that stretched across the state of New York and parts of the provinces of Ontario and Quebec, and together, their decisions had to be unanimous. The sixth nation, the Tuscarora, moved to Iroquois country in the early eighteenth century.

The people of the Confederacy developed a brilliant way of arriving at decisions. The Great Council was made up of chiefs who were selected by the women of the community. At council, the Onondaga introduced an issue and offered it to the Mohawk for consideration. When a decision was reached, they passed it to the Seneca. Across a fire, their joint decision was deliberated further, before all the groups. When they reached an agreement,

they reported to the Onondaga Council Leader. If he agreed, the decision was unanimous. If not, the negotiation process began again with the Mohawk. If the Great Council could not come to a unanimous decision, they set aside the matter and covered the fire with ashes. The gathering ended with the acts of council being recorded for posterity in belts of wampum.

Those who crafted the democratic government of the United States, including Benjamin Franklin and Thomas Jefferson, drew inspiration from the Confederacy and its system of government.

To this day, Iroquois law remains unchanged and guides the Grand Council of the People of the Longhouse.

ACKNOWLEDGMENTS

I have read and listened to many versions of this story, but it was Ronwaniente Jocks's telling that brought it to life for me. Thank you. *Nia Wen.*

A special thank you to my models, Grand Chief Joseph Tokwiro Norton and Ka'nahsohn Deer. *Nia wen.*